THE BEDOUIN BOY

Chapter 1 A Trip to the Doctor 2

Chapter 2 A Debt to Pay 12

Chapter 3 The Plan 22

Glossary 32

Written by
ELLEN LEWIS

Illustrations by
MAX STASIUK

Pioneer Valley Educational Press, Inc.

CHAPTER 1
A Trip to the Doctor

"Make sure you hold on tight," said Yousuf.

"I'm going to beat you to the bottom!" cried his younger sister, Dalida.

Sliding down the 100-foot sand dunes was their favorite desert game. **Bedouins** (*BED-wins*) called them the "singing dunes." When the sand rubbed together, it made a humming sound.

Dalida grabbed the sides of her rug and inched herself over the peak. "Here I go!" she yelled.

Yousuf watched his sister and smiled.

Yousuf and Dalida's parents glanced up from their camp near the bottom of the dune. Old Malloof, the family camel, looked up as well, snorting loudly.

Dalida pushed off and raced toward them. Yousuf waited for a few seconds, watching her slide down the dune.

"Yee!" shouted Yousuf as he pushed himself over the edge of the dune. He was a few yards behind his sister. On the way down, the wind and sand flew in their faces.

"I won!" Dalida yelled when she got to the bottom. She stood up and dusted the hot sand off her long blue dress. Then she rubbed her head and coughed.

"What's the matter?" asked Yousuf.

"I don't know," she said. "I feel funny. I think I'm getting sick." Her face was turning red and her eyes began to water. She coughed again.

They walked over to the campfire. Mother felt Dalida's head and said she had a fever. She made Dalida lie down on her sleeping rug inside the tent. Dalida coughed again and again.

That night, Mother treated Dalida with tea made from special leaves, herbs, and seeds. She drank the tea, but the desert medicine didn't seem to help the cough.
The next day she struggled to breathe.

Everyone was worried, and Father made the decision: The family would go into town to see the doctor. They packed the tent and loaded Malloof with their few belongings. Then they went on their journey.

The family did not like to leave the desert. They were Bedouins, living and sleeping in simple tents in the middle of the Arabian Desert. The noise and crowds of people in towns made them uncomfortable.

Dalida was very weak when they arrived in the seaside town three days later. They made their way to the clinic.

The doctors were kind and treated Dalida immediately. The family set up their tent at the edge of town and waited for her to get better. Mother sat with her the whole time while Yousuf, Father, and Grandfather explored the town.

At the **souk** (*sook*), merchants sold all kinds of things, like spices, clothes, pots, and jewels. There were also many pearls. The merchants called out as Yousuf, Father, and Grandfather walked past. The noise sounded like thunder in their ears.

At the harbor, they saw a father and son rowing a boat back to shore. Inside the little boat was a basket.

"They must be traders," Father said. "They buy pearls from the divers and sell them in town."

Yousuf remembered the pearls at the souk. They cost more money than he could imagine.

Dalida slowly improved. The doctors cleared her lungs of the cough, and her fever broke.

The family thanked the doctors and paid them what little money they could. Father and Grandfather promised to pay the rest of the money they owed the clinic. The doctors believed they would pay. Bedouins always paid their debts.

CHAPTER 2
A Debt to Pay

The family was happy Dalida was better. They were excited to return to the desert the next day. Grandfather brought back some special ingredients from the souk, and Mother prepared a feast. She filled their bowls with spicy lamb and sweet rice. Yousuf could smell coffee heating on the fire. He saw a pouch of plump dates for dessert.

After dinner, Grandfather played his violin. The family hummed along as he recited Bedouin poems about camels and starry nights.

Growing up, Bedouin children learned poems about stars, sandstorms, and camels. Yousuf's favorite poem was about a camel who saves a family in the desert by finding water for them. He recited the poem as Grandfather played his violin, but he surprised everyone by changing the name of the camel in the poem to Malloof. The family laughed and clapped in delight.

After the poem, Grandfather poured a cup of coffee for Yousuf.

Dalida patted Malloof on the nose, and the camel snorted. Grandfather said, "He says he didn't like the town either."

Everyone laughed.

"You think I'm joking," said Grandfather, "but it's true. He's been with me for 30 years, and we are like brothers."

"I remember when you bought him from **Sheikh** (*Shake*) Ali," said Father.

"I spent all the money I had saved," said Grandfather.

When Grandfather said this, Yousuf noticed that everyone was smiling except for Father.

An hour later, Yousuf lay in bed. Dalida and Grandfather snored loudly from their side of the tent, but Yousuf couldn't sleep. He could hear his parents whispering to each other outside the tent.

"How will we pay the bill?" asked Mother.

"We must sell Malloof," said Father sadly.

Yousuf gasped.

"Is there no other way?" asked Mother.

Father was silent.

"Who will carry our things?" asked Mother.

"We have the goats and sheep," said Father.

Yousuf could not believe what he heard. Mother was right. If they sold Malloof, they would never be able to travel anywhere. They would have a difficult time carrying items to sell at the market.

Yousuf decided that he must help his family. But what could he do? He was a child, not even 12 years old.

He looked up at the sky through a hole in the tent. The stars sparkled like the jewels he'd seen at the souk. This gave him an idea.

CHAPTER 3
The Plan

In the morning, the family shared a breakfast of pancakes and coffee.

"We'll have to make some changes for now," said Father. "I will find someone to buy Malloof."

"We can't sell him!" said Dalida.

"I know you love Malloof," said Mother. "But we must pay our debts."

"Mother is right. We must pay our debts," said Yousuf. "And Dalida is right, too. We cannot sell Malloof."

"What can we do?" asked Dalida.

"I have a plan," said Yousuf.

The family looked at Yousuf with surprise.

"What's your plan?" asked Mother.

"While we waited for Dalida to get better, Father, Grandfather, and I went to the souk, and I saw pearls everywhere. So many people were buying them," said Yousuf.

"You're just a child. You cannot have your own shop," said Father.

"I don't want to *trade* for pearls," said Yousuf. "I want to *dive* for them."

"You are a desert child!" said Father. "You don't even swim!"

"I'll learn," said Yousuf.

"Those ships are no place for a child," said Mother. "Sometimes the men go and don't come back!"

"I'll come back," said Yousuf.

"The boy is right," said Grandfather. "Selling Malloof may help us pay our debt, but we will struggle without him. The family needs our camel."

"Grandfather, you always say that Bedouins do not run from our fears," said Yousuf.

"We face them head-on," said Grandfather.

Mother and Father were quiet for a while. Then Father said, "There is a **Nakhuda** (*na-KOO-da*) in town. I will take Yousuf to meet him."

They returned to town that afternoon. The Nakhuda they met was in charge of a small pearling boat. The Nakhuda looked at Yousuf to see if he was strong enough. Then he handed some **rupees** (*roo-PEES*) to Father.

"This man will train you to dive," said Father to Yousuf.

Yousuf nodded at the captain. "Thank you, sir. I will pack my things."

The Nakhuda pointed at the harbor where the **dhow** (*dow*) rocked in the waves. "That will be your home for the next three months."

Mother's face was wet with tears.

Father and Grandfather looked sad too.

Dalida cried, "No, Yousuf, don't leave us!"

Yousuf leaned down to his sister and said, "I will return soon. And when I do, I will bring you a treasure." He stood up and hugged Mother and Dalida.

The Nakhuda led Yousuf to the dhow. "You're a small boy, and you can't swim. This will not be an easy time for you."

"I am nearly a man," said Yousuf, "and I am a Bedouin. I will do this for my family."

Yousuf gazed at the shimmering blue sea. What was down below the sparkling waters? Did his future lay in the belly of shark or with riches and pearls? He would find out soon enough.

Glossary

Bedouins (*BED-wins*)
means "desert dwellers"; people who live in tents and move throughout the Arabian Desert

dhow (*dow*)
wooden boats in the Arabian Gulf

Nakhuda (*na-KOO-da*)
the captain of a pearling boat

rupees (*roo-PEES*)
units of money in the Arabian Gulf

Sheikh (*shake*)
an Arab leader

souk (*sook*)
a marketplace that sells food, clothing, jewelry, and household items